To Susan and David, who inspire me. — A.B.   To Susan and Perrin. — D.R.

ARTIST'S NOTE

I love hats. I have long admired the fashion editor Isabella Blow, her style and creativity, and the bold and imaginative way she wore hats. Isabella celebrated and inspired designers, and in particular the milliner Philip Treacy, whose amazing creations she wore with finesse.

Having worked as a milliner myself for several years before turning my hand to illustration, I have a particular appreciation for the attention Isabella Blow brought to this art form. I decided to base the character of Madame Chapeau on her and feature many of the extraordinary hats created by Philip Treacy that Isabella was photographed wearing. The hats in this book are some of my personal favorites, not only by Philip Treacy but also by other milliners, including Stephen Jones and Elsa Schiaparelli. I've included a few of my own designs as well.

Some of the iconic hats pictured within include the upturned shoe hat designed by Schiaparelli in the 1930s, showing how surrealism influenced fashion; the Philip Treacy hat worn by Princess Beatrice to the wedding of Prince William and Catherine Middleton; the Treacy pink satin head-dress worn by Grace Jones; the famous derby worn by Charlie Chaplin; and the crumpled top hat worn by the mime artist Marcel Marceau.

Sadly, Isabella Blow died in 2007, but her legacy remains in the tremendous influence she had on fashion and in the work she still inspires in designers and artists today.

Cataloging-in-Publication Data has been applied for and may be obtained from the Library of Congress.

ISBN: 978-1-4197-1219-7

Text copyright © 2014 Andrea Beaty
Illustrations copyright © 2014 David Roberts
Title Typography design by Megan Bennett • Book design by Chad W. Beckerman

Printed and bound in U.S.A.
10 9 8 7 6 5 4 3 2 1

ABRAMS
THE ART OF BOOKS SINCE 1949
115 West 18th Street
New York, NY 10011
www.abramsbooks.com

WORDS BY ANDREA BEATY   PICTURES BY DAVID ROBERTS

HAPPY BIRTHDAY
Madame Chapeau

Abrams Books for Young Readers, New York

In a three-story house with a shop down below

lived the world's finest hatmaker, Madame Chapeau.

Like the lady herself, all her hats were refined—
brilliantly singular, one of a kind!
Each feather, each bauble, each bead, and each bow—
painstakingly chosen by Madame Chapeau.

From promptly at eight till exactly at four,

the hatless but hopeful arrived at her door.

Each person was special. Each one of a kind,

and perfectly matched to the hat she designed.

She made hats for all, from the young to the old,

and each left her boutique a sight to behold.

Then, climbing the stairs with her dog and her cat,
the lonely, shy hatmaker took off her hat.
A sliver of gouda, a plum, and a scone,
the Lady Chapeau ate her dinner alone.

Just one night a year—on her birthday, no less—
the lady unpacked her most elegant dress,
the one with the frills and the frou-frou upon it.

And last but not least chose her best birthday bonnet.
She strolled through the streets in her elegant gown
to dine—all alone—at the best place in town.

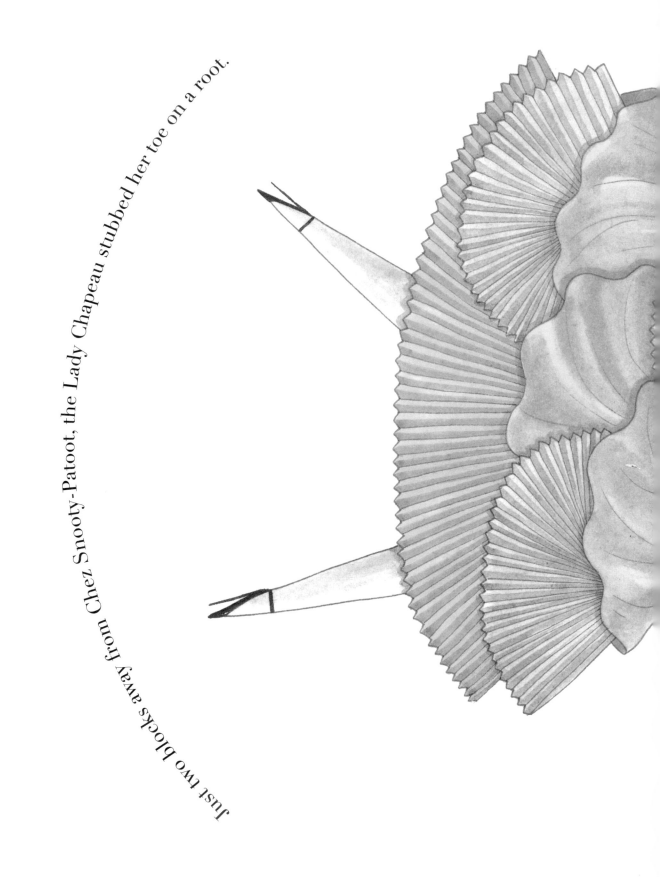

Just two blocks away from Chez Snooty-Patoot, the Lady Chapeau stubbed her toe on a root.

She took a great tumble and flipped head-to-toe. Her fine birthday bonnet was seized by a crow!

"My hat! My hat! Come back with my hat!

You simply can't steal someone's bonnet like that!

Someone quite special once made that for *me*.

You can't steal my hat and fly off to a tree!"

"Madame," said a baker. "Please take my tall hat."

"Oh, thank you, but truly, I couldn't do that!

What would you wear on the top of your head

while baking your biscuits, your scones, and your bread?

No, no, kind monsieur. Someone made that for *you*.

For me to run off with it simply won't do.

Where Avenue Rouge becomes Rue Tippytap,

she met a policeman, who held out his cap.

"Alas," said Madame, "though I do love the look,

you'll need your fine hat when you capture a crook."

"Take mine," said a cowboy (in a Stetson, of course).

But how could she take it? It matched his black horse!

A Scotsman. A jockey. A mime and a spy—

each offered the lady a new hat to try.

She said no to a derby. And no to a fez.

And no to the sombrero of Señor Cortez.

Each hat that she saw was a pitch-perfect fit
for the kind, lovely soul who was perfect for it.
She knew that each hat—with its feathers or fur—
was made for someone who was simply not her.

A very old merchant on Rue Pompadour

with only one hat on the shelves in his store

said, "Take this small present. I think it's just right."

Shyly she smiled. But the hat was too tight.

She blushed a bright pink from her toe to her head.

"Thank you, it's lovely," Madame Chapeau said.

She walked through the town on the long, winding route that came to an end at Chez Snooty-Patoot.

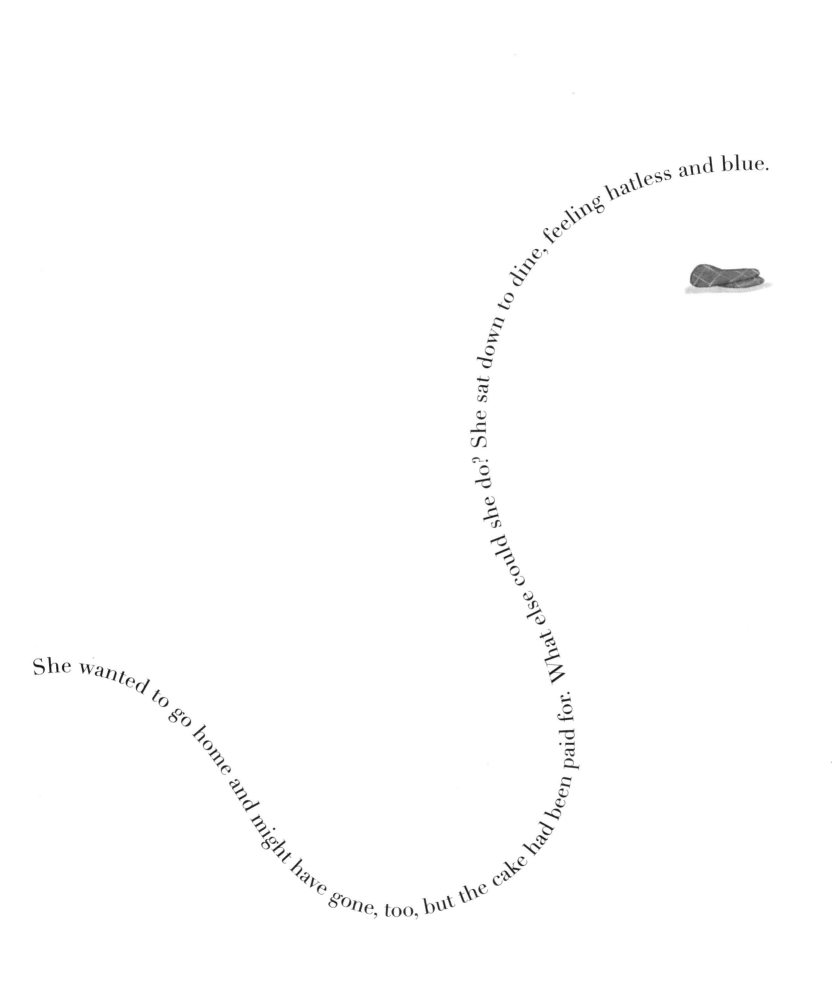

She wanted to go home and might have gone, too, but the cake had been paid for. What else could she do? She sat down to dine, feeling hatless and blue.

The restaurant was crowded and fussy and loud.

The fancy-pants waiters brought dishes and bowed.

The plates were a picture! The souffle a sight!

The hatless hatmaker could not touch a bite.

She sat at her elegant table and sighed.

She looked out the window and quite nearly cried.

"Excuse me, madame," said a girl dressed in plaid.

"I made you a gift from some yarn that I had.

I made it myself, and I just want to say,

I hope you enjoy it . . . and Happy Birthday!"

The girl held a brightly knit cap in her hand,

with thin purple stripes and a wide orange band.

Its earflaps were yellow. Its pom-pom was green.

A freakier headpiece has never been seen.

"It looks rather odd," said the Lady Chapeau.

"This hat has no baubles. No beads. And no bow!

It's stretchy . . . it's cozy . . . it's easy to squish.

It's knitted with love and your best birthday wish!"

"How wonderfully perfect! The right hat for me!

A true birthday bonnet, I'm sure you'll agree!

I thank you so much! And I thank all of you,

so join me for dinner—and chocolate cake, too!"

They feasted on gateau and sorbet with fruit
and danced through the night at Chez Snooty-Patoot.
Then Madame Chapeau wore her birthday hat home.
And never again did she dine all alone.